THE STEWARDESS'S DIARY - PART SIX

THAILAND

S.M. PRATT

The Stewardess's Diary - Part Six: Thailand
Copyright © 2016 by S.M. Pratt

This is a work of fiction. Names, characters, businesses, places, events, and incidents are either the products of the author's imagination or used in a fictitious manner. Any resemblance to actual persons, living or dead, or actual events is purely coincidental.

WARNING: This is a work of erotic fiction and contains GRAPHIC DEPICTIONS OF SEX, WHICH MAY OFFEND SOME AUDIENCES. This book is meant for MATURE AUDIENCES AGED 18 OR OLDER (or whatever the local laws are in your area). All sexually active characters in this work are 18 years of age or older.

Last updated January 25th, 2020
Editing by Samantha Marie

ISBN: 978-0-9940630-9-0 (e-book)

ISBN: 978-1-988639-25-3 (paperback)

I'M CHARLIE, a veteran pilot for a major international airline that shall remain nameless for reasons you'll soon come to understand.

A year ago, while waiting for my flight to London in the airline's lounge at one of America's largest hubs, I discovered a special and highly personal journal among my belongings. How it happened, I'll never know, but the beautiful brown leather notebook nonetheless appeared in my briefcase at some point between the time I left my New York penthouse apartment and arrived at the airport lounge.

Perhaps it was a mix-up at security, or some devious stewardess with sly hand skills, but I've since become obsessed with the person who wrote that diary, her stories, and—to be blunt—her unconventional sex life.

My best friend—let's call him Bob—is one of my regular co-pilots. Bob advised me to forget about the journal and ignore my hunch to track down its rightful owner. After my initial reading of her hand-written accounts, the part of me who's loyal to the airline and wants the best for our passengers certainly needed to find that stewardess and expel her from our company—or whatever airline she's with. This woman is surely a threat to any crew with her irreverent disregard for our uniforms, her sexual behavior with passengers and airline employees, and the way she ignores regulations. She should clearly be punished for her conduct...

But after reading and re-reading each one of her journal entries, another, more animal part of me has grown fond of her complete lack of boundaries, her willingness to experiment, and her ravenous sexual appetite.

I've had my fair share of illicit affairs with female flight attendants and co-pilots, but none of them were interesting enough to be granted a second fuck by yours truly, let alone be courted or considered for a long-term relationship. But the woman who's filled so many pages with delicate calligraphy and salacious words deserves my full attention. She's certainly maintained it well past the time I closed the cover of her journal—again and again.

Imagining how her naiveté was gradually—and most willingly—robbed from her was simply... enthralling. She's been haunting my wet dreams.

Now, every time I see an unknown stewardess, I wonder if *she's* the one.

After many conversations with Bob over the past months during our overseas flights, I've come to share some of her journal entries with him. He agrees that I need to locate her. If not for the airline's sake or to satisfy my personal curiosity, then for the mere reason that I could stop obsessing about her and resume paying attention to my actual job: piloting giant aircrafts and safely getting passengers from point A to point B.

The following short stories record my obsession toward her. There are ten in total. Each installment contains my mystery stewardess's original journal entries for a specific location, followed by my own experiences in trying to track her down. You'll discover what (and whom) I did in an effort to identify and locate my stewardess based on the clues she's left in her diary. You can read the episodes in any order, but they'll probably make more sense if you start from the beginning and follow along as I attempt to find her.

And, just to be clear, these stories should *not* land in the hands of any prude or underage person. Some are just romantic, sensual, or highly erotic, while others are immoral, perverse, and possibly even illegal in some parts of the world.

Ah, the things I'll do to this mystery stewardess when I finally encounter her in the flesh!

I'm hard just thinking about it...

Yours truly,

Capt. Charlie
Undisclosed Airline

PART ONE

THE STEWARDESS'S
ENTRIES

6:12 A.M.

AFTER TURNING on the lights and making the morning announcements in both Thai and English, Ellie came to chat with me in the galley at the back of the plane.

It was my first time working with her. She was the living incarnation of sweetness, politeness, and cordiality with every guest and flight attendant. Since I'd discovered (during our pre-flight meeting) we'd both be spending a few days in Bangkok, we'd been using our few minutes of downtime here and there to get to know each other a bit more. She didn't talk about herself much, though. And it's not like I loved talking about myself either... but not answering her questions would have been impolite.

So we ended up mostly chatting about me, then about nothing and everything, except her.

Maybe she's just shy.

However, I wanted to ask her one specific question, but I'd yet to find a way to phrase it without sounding strange or rude. Ellie looked like a mini Thai Barbie (if such a thing existed). She had that weird big-breast to small-waist/small-hip ratio that the famous doll portrayed. I couldn't say that I'd come across many big-breasted Asian women before.

She has to have had a boob job, no?

READY FOR THE flight's final food service, I followed Ellie with the cart down the port aisle. She looked as fresh and energetic as someone who'd just woken up from a ten-hour sleep in the world's most comfortable bed.

As she walked backward to the front of the economy section, pulling the cart while I pushed it, I couldn't help but stare at her pale—probably cosmetically-bleached—skin, her shiny, silky black hair, and her impressively large breasts for such narrow hips. The short-sleeved white uniform blouse she wore had to have been tailored especially for her.

Ellie and I began offering hot breakfast to the

economy folks sitting on our side of the plane, starting with those at the front. We slowly handed out small plastic trays to our sleepy, red-eyed passengers. They got to choose between a tomato-and-cheese omelet or French toast, and both were accompanied by yogurt, orange juice, and a two-bite fruit salad. We then offered hot coffee or tea prior to moving our attention to the next row. Slowly but surely, we made our way toward the back of the plane. Ellie served those in the front while I attended to the rows behind the cart.

After taking 34A's drink order, Ellie called out to me, so I turned my attention to her. She gave a slight head nudge toward the man sitting right next to where she stood while pouring hot coffee into a disposable cup.

Curious, I paused my service and looked at the blond man. I couldn't see much from where I stood, but his medium-length hair and the profile of his nose and jaw made me realize who he was. I'd spotted him when he'd boarded. Handsome would have been an under qualifier for this man. I looked at Ellie again.

She stretched her upper body across the other two passengers sitting between her and the woman who was sitting by the window. "Here you go, ma'am," said Ellie, her large breasts coming less than an inch from handsome 34C's face as she delivered the woman's drink.

She moved out of the passengers' way and smiled at 34C. "Sorry for my reach," she said.

"No problem at all," said the blond man before pushing the button on his armrest to straighten the back of his seat, which made his upper body move forward a bit. *Is he hoping for seconds with 34B's upcoming drink delivery?*

"Green tea?" asked 34B, an older Asian man who looked up from his food tray just long enough to make his request.

Ellie made 34B's drink, then winked at 34C while she served 34B his tea. No boob contact, but I swear she overfilled 34B's cup just so she could deliver it super slowly to grant 34C more time to stare at her breasts. *Man, she's smooth!*

Drink delivered without a drip, she looked at the handsome blond man again. He cleared his throat then asked, "Black coffee, and do you have any salty snacks left-over from the previous service?"

Ellie looked at me with a large smile before replying, "Let me check." She motioned for me to back the cart a bit, then adjusted her scarf to clear the front of her cleavage.

I backed the cart as she'd requested, even though we didn't have anything but breakfast trays in the slots and hot drinks on top. *What is she doing?*

She bent down and rummaged through the trays, looking for snacks that both she and I knew were not there. But 34C's eyes were glued on her cleavage. She was obviously taking her sweet time and enjoying the man's attention.

36A cleared her throat next to me, so I turned to her and handed her the breakfast tray I'd been holding in the air for nearly a minute now.

8:52 A.M.

ELLIE and I helped the last passenger off the plane: an elderly American woman who'd told us she was traveling on her own, hoping to visit as many countries as possible before kicking her ultimate bucket. *Is this what I'll become? Is she a future version of me?*

She wore a loose-fitting, flowing dress with a paisley pattern, which gave her a hippy look. Her long gray hair was tied in a braid; she didn't seem to wear any make up, save for a pale shade of shiny pink on her lips. *Traveling the world solo as an elderly woman would certainly beat sitting around in a retirement home and playing bingo with a bunch of grumpy, bitchy women with white-blue hair who do nothing but compete to get the attention of one of the rare few remaining men. Traveling would open the door to a lot more options...*

A few minutes later, having tidied up the plane and ensured nothing had been left behind by the passengers, Ellie and I headed toward customs, chit-chatting about Bangkok, our carry-ons in tow. She'd grown up in the capital and was excited to have the opportunity to share her knowledge of the city with me.

"Why don't you follow me to my favorite hotel? It's clean and inexpensive. Maybe we can have a short nap and then you can put on something pretty? I can take you out this afternoon and show you around town?"

"Sounds like a plan!" I said, looking forward to resting for a couple of hours.

THE AIR in Bangkok was heavy and smoggy. Much muggier than I had remembered and anticipated.

Thankfully, the hotel Ellie and I went to offered air-conditioned rooms. After a short nap, I felt re-energized, at least enough to dig through my carry-on and remind myself of the clothes I had packed. I didn't have many options, but since Ellie said to wear something pretty, I skipped my jeans—it was way too hot for those anyway—and settled on my burnt-orange, button-down sundress with a pair of comfortable yet feminine sandals.

I had a quick look at myself in the mirror. The chiffon-nylon fabric ended about an inch lower than the middle of my thighs, which was a good length for me. However, my bra straps showed, clashing with the outfit. *Should I go braless?* I took it off, then looked at myself again. *Much better, but will I attract too much attention?*

I took a few steps back, then walked forward toward the mirror, paying attention to my chest as I advanced. Sure, my breasts were not hanging by my belly button—I had to admit they were still quite perky, especially in this air-conditioned room—but the light, flowing fabric of my dress followed my breasts as they swayed unrestricted with each step. *Don't breast tissues benefit when women go braless? Or will it offend local people?* I definitely didn't want to cause any cultural discomfort if it could be avoided by wearing a bra, even though the straps were unsightly at best.

I put my bra back on and opened my bedroom door to head out into the hallway when I saw Ellie standing in front of me, her arm raised as though she was about to knock. She wore an outfit that reminded me of a Japanese school girl. She'd donned a white shirt tied in a knot around her tiny waist, exposing her flat stomach. Her belly button was decorated by a silver ring. Her breasts pushed the blouse's semi-sheer fabric to the extreme; two buttons barely kept the blouse closed over her bright, lime-green bra. She'd kept her stewardess neck scarf and had added a short pleated skirt and long white socks to her look. *Most men would probably want a piece of that!*

"Hi," I said.

She lowered her arm and smiled at me. "Ready?" she asked.

I pointed at my shoulders. "I'm unsure about my straps."

She looked at me. A tiny vertical line appeared between her brows as she shook her head. "It's a really pretty dress, but those straps..."

"Okay," I said, relieved that my initial guess was right. *Better fix my outfit now.* I invited her to come in, then closed the door behind her.

I unclasped my bra through the fabric of my dress before taking it off. After contorting my arms around the dress's spaghetti straps, I tossed the unneeded garment on my bed, then readjusted the dress's straps before looking at myself in the mirror again. *Much better.*

I turned to face Ellie. "But do you think it's too much if I walk around like this?" I asked her while trotting around the room, probably a little faster than I'd be walking anyway, but my breasts really bouncing with each step.

She shook her head. "No problem." The large smile she'd displayed throughout the entire flight had reappeared. "You're much prettier without the ugly straps."

"But this won't offend anyone?" I asked.

She raised her shoulders. "If they're offended, they can look elsewhere. We're not going to visit a temple. What really offends Thai people is tourists who point their feet at them or at monks... or at Buddha statues. You're ready now?"

I nodded.

"Let's go," she said, walking out of my room. "We're going to have fun today, right?"

"Sure," I said, looking forward to being led by this exotic little thing on our upcoming tour of her native Bangkok.

I locked my door, then followed her into the hallway, my small purse in hand.

"Are you hungry?" she asked as we stepped into the elevator.

"A little," I replied, surprised by my stomach, which growled in agreement.

"First we feed your belly, then your mind. After that? Party time!"

"Why not? Let's do it!" I had no idea what she meant by *feeding my mind* since she'd already said we weren't going to visit a temple, but it didn't matter anyway. I was certain Ellie would show me a good time.

We stepped out of the elevator, then left the hotel and hit the streets.

Ellie hailed a *tuk-tuk*. She said something to the driver in Thai, then we got in the three-wheeled motorcycle taxi, which soon merged into traffic, sputtering loudly as the driver weaved his way to our destination, whatever it was.

I couldn't read (or speak) Thai, so I relied on what Ellie told me, especially since she'd promised we'd head out, away from the popular tourist traps.

1:10 P.M.

WE SPENT an hour at a food market. The smells were out of this world. *I wish I could just bottle this sweet and spicy aroma and bring it back with me in my suitcase.* There was something about Thai food I'd always loved. Some vendors grilled fish, others offered roasted duck and chicken. Of course, there were lots of soups, noodles, and curries to pick from as well. After our initial stroll through the market, Ellie and I settled on eating a green mango salad, *moo ping* (grilled pork skewers), shrimp pad thai, and a little bit of fresh (and very stinky) durian for dessert.

"Are you thirsty?" Ellie asked while getting rid of our empty food containers.

"Yes, quite a bit actually."

"I know a very special tea room. It's just around the corner from here."

I would have settled for a stop at the nearest shop or vendor stand to pick up an ice-cold bottle of *Est* Cola, but tea was probably healthier. "Sounds good."

I readjusted my sandal strap, then followed Ellie down the busy street. Her tiny school-girl outfit had certainly caught the eyes of more than a handful of men as she strolled away, a few feet ahead of me.

A WALL LINED with various glass jars stood behind the man at the counter in the shop we'd just walked in. Some were nearly full, others nearly empty. They all contained loose tea leaves, herbs, roots, dried mushrooms, or dried fruit. The shop attendant exchanged a few words with Ellie, then she winked at him and leaned on the high counter, her huge breasts resting on it. The Thai man did not even bother being discreet about eying her oversized cleavage. After whispering something to him, she slipped him a few bills. He grabbed them so quickly I wasn't able to see how many *bahts* she'd spent. He stuffed the money in the till, then headed to the back, leaving us and the other customers waiting.

Two minutes later, he came back with a steaming teapot and two cups on a tray.

"Now, let's go and get ourselves seated," Ellie said, walking toward the back of the shop, where a couple was just leaving.

The hot beverage was a little strange tasting. More bitter than green tea, yet fruitier at the same time. It quenched my thirst, but it also made me feel more rested, more open-minded, and more curious about the world around me. An irrepressible need to examine the painting that hung close to my head came over me. A super-fat, super-happy Buddha had been hand-painted in shades of yellow, pink, and green. Once I'd taken in all the gorgeous details and paint strokes, I returned my attention to Ellie and suddenly noticed the tiny freckles on her cheeks.

"How are you doing?" she asked just as a man poured more steamy water into our teapot.

"Very relaxed yet energized. Isn't it strange? I'm normally exhausted after a fifteen-hour flight, but I'm... full of energy," I said.

"Excellent, your mind has been fed! Let's finish

this teapot, then we'll head out for a spa treatment and massage. How does that sound?"

"Like pure heaven," I replied, suddenly realizing how much I was craving physical contact. Even the feel of my own fingers mindlessly brushing my forearm was amazing right now. I could imagine 34C's hands on my shoulders, rubbing away the pain of a long day. He could rub me elsewhere, too, and maybe prod me a little... or a lot... My insides twitched in agreement. I closed my eyes for a few seconds, imagining what 34C would feel like in me... But when I felt blood rush to my face, I suddenly became afraid that I'd just let out a loud moan for the entire tea room to hear.

I looked around. Nobody was staring at me. *Good!*

Ellie pushed her chair away from the table, then got up.

"You're ready now! Let's go."

I'm ready? How would she know if I no longer wanted any more tea? But I was certainly craving that massage now. It had been a while since I'd splurged.

I downed what was left of my cup, got up, and then followed Ellie out of the tea shop.

ELLIE HAILED ANOTHER *TUK-TUK*. About fifteen minutes later, we once again left the hot and humid air of Bangkok's streets behind us. But this time, it was to enter a spa.

A small two-tiered fountain gurgled in the middle of the entrance, and the sounds of singing monks filled the incense-laden air. A handsome, young man stood behind the front desk, and a short woman with silky black hair wearing a matching white linen uniform was escorting a thin, gray-haired client to another section of the building, past the fountain.

"Ellie!" the man exclaimed before running

around the counter, wrapping his arms around her, and then lifting her up in the air.

"Chakrii," she said once he finally let her down, "this is my friend. She needs... a special spa treatment. Can you arrange this for us?"

The man eyed me up and down, as though his black eyes could read my mind and figure out if I wanted a facial or a body wrap. But I swear he paused for a second or two on my breasts. I looked down. A big, wet horizontal line was visible on the orange fabric, just below my breasts. *Probably from sitting and sweating in the* tuk-tuk *too long...* Back home, I would have been a little embarrassed, but it was freaking hot and humid in this country. *Can't blame myself for perspiring!*

"May I see your list of services?" I asked him, wiping sweat off my brow. My own hand felt a little foreign on my face. *Am I getting heat stroke? No... Just a little buzzed. But from what?*

"Of course," he said before walking back toward the counter.

When he returned, he handed me a one-page leaflet with a list of spa treatments offered by the *Shave, Massage, and Beyond Spa*, along with their respective prices. He then added, "And we offer whatever other services you may need." As he finished his sentence in perfect, near-unaccented English, his hand wiped a drop of sweat that was making its way down my cleavage. A small tattoo of a flower adorned his index finger, which was a tad delicate for a man's, but his touch sent a tingling ripple down my spine nonetheless.

I smiled and let out a nervous laugh. Chakrii was probably one of the better-looking Thai men I'd seen to date. Tall, tanned, his hair neatly kept, a charming smile, and black eyes that were currently locked onto mine. I almost dared undoing the top two or three buttons of my dress just so I could feel more of his touch. I was sure more and more sweat would trickle down, but I restrained myself. I had to put my horniness aside for now. "Let me have a look," I finally said, looking at the leaflet and feeling a wave of arousal engulf me.

The full Brazilian wax and full-body massage seemed quite appealing at this very moment. I'd never had a Brazilian wax before, but why not give it a try? If I didn't like it, I could just keep my bald pussy to myself until I could grow my regular narrow strip again.

"I want the Brazilian wax and full-body massage," I told Chakrii.

"Sounds like fun," said Ellie. "I'll get the same. Can you book us together?" she asked.

Although she hadn't checked with me first, I was fine with it.

"Of course, Ellie. Anything for you, you know that." Chakrii turned his attention to me. "Please wait here," he said, pointing to a couple of chairs facing the fountain, "and someone will be right with the both of you."

"Exciting," Ellie said, grabbing my hand and pulling me to the waiting area. "You'll love him... it," she corrected herself before winking at me. "I just know it."

2:50 P.M.

A SHORT BUT muscular man who wore the spa's white linen uniform bowed at us with the symbolic *wai*. "Please follow me to the shower and change room," he said.

Ellie and I got up. He led us into a wide-open, circular area surrounded by thin white linen curtains that danced in an invisible breeze. A huge fan hung high in the center of the ceiling. The humongous device was responsible for the delightful breeze that was now cooling my overheated body. Right below the ceiling fan stood a tall and wide pillar with a few shower heads peppered around its circumference. Water currently spurted out of them like rain showers. The room itself looked like an oversized water fountain. The shower's circular floor was tiled with tiny black and white squares and enclosed within a foot-high rim, which served to keep some water in the lower basin.

"Please wash up, then put on a robe," he said, first pointing at the pillar in front of us, then moving his hand to indicate the rack of towels and silk robes that hung in various sizes across the room from us. "You can leave your clothes and valuables in one of the lockers on your right. Don't worry, your things will be safe here."

Taking a communal shower was new to me, but I was hot and sweaty. And I'd grown quite comfortable with my body over the past months. Plus, the only other person in the room was Ellie. If she saw me in the buff, that would mean I'd get to see her naked, too. I'd finally know the answer to the question that had puzzled me since I first saw her. I looked around and the muscular man seemed to have quietly disappeared. He was nowhere to be seen.

Ellie stored her purse in one of the small lockers, then took off her shoes and socks. I followed her lead. She then jumped into the fountain-style shower without even removing her scarf, blouse, or skirt. She let me finish taking off my sandals, but then ran back up to me and dragged me under the stream of water with my dress still on.

"Isn't this fun?" she asked.

I had to agree. It was as though we'd backtracked in time; we'd morphed into two younger girls who were now doing what adults claimed was not appropriate. Ellie let go of my hands, then leaned her head back, letting the stream of water wash over her sheer white blouse, making it even more transparent. She pulled back her long, shiny, black hair, letting the water soak it, then flipped it repeatedly like a dog shaking itself dry, except that it was her huge boobs bouncing left and right that got my attention, not her long, wet hair that had sprayed me in the process. She untied the knot in her shirt below her breasts and undid her buttons. The fabric finally got a rest from its overextension. She slowly pulled the wet blouse away from her body, as if she was giving a show to a large audience at a strip club.

She was freaking sexy in that lacy green bra. I envied her breasts and how much sensuality oozed out of her.

After throwing her blouse on the floor a few feet away from us, out of the basin, she came toward me, then brought me back with her under the fountain's lukewarm stream.

"Close your eyes," she ordered before lifting up my chin, removing my hair clip, and then running her fingers through my wet hair. "Doesn't this feel good?" she asked.

All I could do was smile. The water hit me at just the perfect temperature and pressure: it cooled me off and teased me at the same time. Ellie's fingers went down from the crown of my head to my face to my neck. After pausing for a second, she slowly unbuttoned the front of my dress, as if she was enjoying every titillating second.

When I opened my eyes, all of my buttons were undone. Ellie was kneeling in front of me, her head aligned with my crotch. She wrapped her hands around my knees then slid them up along the outside of my thighs, grabbing a feel of my ass quickly thereafter. Her soft touch was just what I craved this minute. I couldn't wait to enjoy what the upcoming whole-body massage would feel like. Ellie pulled her hands away from me before standing up.

"Let's have a look at you," she said before peeling off one side of my dress and exposing my left breast.

"Even more beautiful than I imagined," she

said. She traced the shape of my exposed breast with her finger then looked down at my wet panties. "White, just like I thought."

"Why?" I asked.

"You come across as a very... innocent woman," she said, smiling at me before peeling off the other side of my dress. "What's the expression? The girl next door?"

I let her rhetorical question be while she turned me around. She pulled off my drenched orange dress before tossing it near her blouse, outside of the basin.

Now wearing nothing but my panties, I arched my back and enjoyed the way each water droplet landed on my exposed breasts. I was definitely buzzed on something. Didn't know what, though. I hadn't smoked anything. And I don't think food poisoning had ever had that kind of pleasant effect... It had to have been the tea. Each water droplet from the shower felt like it had been imbued with some sort of super power to both cool me and caress me. But it wasn't just that. It was as though every single thing that touched my skin sent a large ripple that reverberated all the way down to my pussy. I was horny as hell. I craved physical contact. And there I was... showering next to a beautiful, big-breasted woman who still wore a few more layers than me. I wanted Ellie as much as any man I could get my hands on. *34C would be so useful right about now...*

Ellie reached behind her back and undid her bra. Her perky, globular girls bounced out in the world just inches from my eyes. They were simply too round to be true. I finally let out the question I'd been meaning to ask ever since I saw her. "Are they natural?"

"Are you kidding? Hell no!" Ellie grabbed both of my hands and placed them right on her breasts, forcing me to squeeze them tight. "Do you like them?"

As though my brain no longer controlled my limbs, I kept touching them, squeezing them, kneading them. They were so firm, yet so soft; her dark nipples were so small, yet the amount of soft, light flesh around them was unbelievable.

"Got them last year. A gift to myself, along with my new hair extensions. What do you think?" she asked, pushing her chest out even more while I kept fondling her.

"Wow," is all I got out.

She reached for my natural breasts. Her hands were much more gentle with mine than I was with hers. She rolled one of my nipples between her fingers. My breathing sped up and my chest started moving up and down much more rapidly. I closed my eyes for a few delightful seconds, then opened them again, feeling as though someone was spying on us. I looked toward the curtains in front of me: a pair of feet was visible at their base. When the fan-induced breeze once again lifted the light fabric, I recognized the short muscular man.

"I think he's waiting for us," Ellie said. She took her hands away from my breasts. "One more thing, and you'll be ready to go."

What now?

She once again knelt in front of me, but this time, her fingers slid into the sides of my panties. She pushed them down to my ankles with her face not even an inch from my wet pussy. I lifted my feet to step out of my underwear, then she tossed it out of the basin.

"And let's not forget to get you clean, too. The massage will feel so much nicer, I swear," she said before getting up, turning around, and then walking toward the soap dispenser on the center pillar.

A few seconds later, Ellie came back to me with a handful of light blue liquid. Still wearing her scarf and her skirt, she made the soap foam in her hands before washing my hair, massaging my scalp, and then rinsing my hair. I grabbed some of the soap to wash my face. Removing a layer of pollution from my skin had never felt so good.

While I closed my eyes to rinse away the suds from my face, I felt Ellie's hands on my breasts. I stepped away from the stream, and she got more soap. A moment later, she started lathering my womanhood, my trimmed pussy hair helping to create more foam. And—I had to be honest—hair had started to regrow around my landing strip. Maintaining my pubic 'do seemed like a full-time job at times. Ellie stood in front of me and let her hand slip down between my legs. Her breasts were against mine, her soapy fingers sliding slowly up and down around my private folds. Without warning, she slapped me on the ass before pushing me down to sit in the shallow water. A second later, she joined me on the floor. Her fingers brushed back and forth between my lips, quickly and firmly. Then, as though nothing but mechanical tasks had happened, she stared at me right in the eyes and said, "Good to go."

She stood up and helped me get on my feet. A second later, she playfully pushed me away from her, toward the towels and robes. "Dry yourself up and follow him. I'll be right with you," she said, a large smile on her face.

By the time she'd finished her sentence, the short, muscular spa employee had stepped up next to me. He extended a towel like a barrier between the two of us. I turned 180 degrees and he wrapped the thick, luscious fabric around me before patting me dry. He wasn't feeling me up per se, but it still felt good.

A couple of minutes later, he let my towel drop to the floor. He then handed me a short white robe that I would have described as a silk kimono. Nothing like the plush robes normally used in spas. The fabric felt so smooth and soft against my skin. I almost felt naked with the robe on since the fabric was so thin and so short; it ended just an inch or so below my pussy.

I turned around and saw Ellie, still enjoying the shower, her hands soaping her huge breasts sensually.

Right now, I wouldn't mind doing her.

I FOLLOWED the short man into another circular room, which was also surrounded by linen curtains.

No fan hung from the ceiling this time, but a large one was resting on a low stand on the floor next to two strange-looking massage chairs. They were angled away from each other and looked as though the makers had incorporated features from a dentist's chair, a massage table, and a gynecologist's exam area. The chairs had the regular padded hole where the patrons' faces could rest when lying on their stomach, but they were currently angled, and they each had two foot rests like an ob-gyn's exam table. With the number of sticks and levers below the center of the chairs, they could probably be repositioned to be flat like regular massage tables when needed.

"We'll start with the Brazilian wax," he said. With his hand, he indicated the first chair. "Do you want a mild analgesic to dull the pain?"

Because I was unsure of what would follow— having never had the wax procedure done before but having heard horror tales—I agreed to his analgesic offer. I sat down with my legs together, hanging between the foot rests.

He acknowledged my reply, then exited the room, leaving me alone to think.

Where's Ellie? Still cleaning herself up in the shower?

Wasn't it strange that seeing her exposed breasts —and imagining her under the shower right now— could turn me on so much?

...And it wasn't the first time a hot woman had had that effect on me. I often thought about those two blondes in Mexico...

Does this mean I'm officially bi?

When my short masseur came back about a minute later, he rolled a low stool in front of my dangling legs. He wrapped one hand around my left ankle and lifted it to the closest foot rest before tying it in place with a piece of pink silk fabric. He repeated with my other ankle, leaving my legs parted like a woman who was about to deliver a baby. I looked at myself: the short silk kimono no longer covered anything below my loosely-tied belt. I saw that the short man had brought along a small tray with him. My legs were parted wide enough for him to roam free between the tray and my pussy.

After warning me that the cream may feel a little cool, his gloved hand spread a thick layer of it over anything and everything that had hair down there. "It will take a few minutes to work," he said with a smile. "Would you like a cup of tea while we wait?"

"Why not," I replied, realizing I was indeed thirsty.

He left me alone once more. It was strange to just sit there, with my legs wide open and pussy exposed, but it wasn't like I was going to undo my ankle ties and make him re-tie them again. My inner prude forced me to bring my knees closer together for a few seconds, but the new position was uncomfortable, so I let my thighs drop to their previous positions. My pussy was again wide open for business. Images of handsome 34C floated on my mental canvas, and I wondered what he'd do to me if he were to walk in here and see me in this inviting position.

MY SHORT SPA attendant came back a few minutes later, tea tray in hand, and Ellie in tow.

She too wore the same white, short-sleeved, silk robe, although hers looked a little longer on her shorter body. Her soaking wet hair rested on her right shoulder, making her beautiful dark nipple greet anyone glancing her way.

"More tea. Great!" she said, taking two cups and handing me one. She then walked toward the second chair and sat down. The way the chairs were positioned, my head was close to hers, but her legs dangled away from my sight. We were near enough to chat, yet our intimate parts were hidden from each other.

The short woman I'd seen before came in and greeted her. "Wax?"

"Yes, please. Take everything off," Ellie ordered the woman who took a seat on a rolling stool.

"No pain killer?" the woman asked Ellie.

"No need. I'm used to it," Ellie replied.

The man between my legs suddenly asked, "Do you feel this?"

"No. What?" I looked down between my legs. He was pinching one of my outer lips.

"Perfect," he said. "I'll get started."

"They use a very strong numbing cream. You won't feel a thing," Ellie said, reassuring me.

I watched the man dip a small wooden stick into a hot container of wax. He applied it to a small area before posing a strip of muslin paper over it. He rolled out of the way, then moved the fan so it now aimed directly at my wide-open legs, saying it helped cool the wax faster.

A few seconds later, he sat back between my legs and snatched the strip of fabric off. As promised, I didn't feel anything down below, even though the ripping sound I'd heard made me believe I should be in a lot of pain. The only thing I could feel was the breeze against my silk robe, my erect nipples announcing the cooler temperature to the world. I slowly sipped my tea while the short muscular man worked his painless magic and bared my groin of hair one strip at a time.

"Do you want your armpits done as well?" the man asked me once he was done with my Brazilian wax, which took a lot less time than I had anticipated.

I had shaved my legs in the shower yesterday before work, but I'd obviously missed my armpits. Suddenly embarrassed that I had unknowingly let my hair grow for a few days—and walked around like that—I agreed.

He took away my empty teacup then tied both of my wrists together with a silk pink ribbon above my head. I could no longer move my arms. I didn't know what he'd tied them to, but I looked at Ellie's chair next to me and saw a small piece of rounded metal that stuck out past the head of her chair. Mine probably had one, too.

"I've applied numbing cream there as well. Let me know when you stop feeling the breeze on your armpits," he said before getting up and walking away from me. The short but very wide sleeves of my kimono had dropped and piled on my shoulders. The ample sleeve gaps had granted lots of room for him to cover my armpits with his pain-numbing cream. I suddenly felt the fan's direction being changed and aimed at my side. The strong breeze forced one side of my kimono to open and flap loosely.

Five minutes later, my armpits were numb—not to mention how cool and perky my exposed right breast was. The same short masseur rolled next to me again and waxed my left armpit clear of hair, then he rolled to the other side and repeated the procedure.

"You're good to go," he said right after he finished. "We'll just wait for the numbing sensation to dissipate before starting your massage. We wouldn't want you to miss any of it." A large smile decorated his face. "I've applied another cream to speed up recovery."

He rolled away from me, leaving me tied up and unable to do anything, save for watching him move the fan back to its previous position. Its strong breeze was once again aimed at my bare pussy, which pushed the other side of my robe away from my body, exposing my other breast.

"I'm all done," I heard Ellie say from the chair next to me. "I'll wait until you're ready, and we'll get our massages at the same time."

"Okay," I said.

I waited. There wasn't much else I could do right now. The light breeze caressed my chest and stomach like a kiss from heaven. Looking at my own body made me feel very sexy. I was a sitting duck— and a horny one at that. My wrists and ankles were tied, my legs wide open, my breasts and pussy exposed. With the fan aimed straight at me, I closed my eyes and imagined 34C gently blowing on my pussy, his fingers reaching for my inner thighs, touching me. I could picture his digits gliding between my folds. I could feel myself getting wet. I spent the next few minutes imagining what he'd do to me and how he'd caress my body, paying particular attention to my pussy.

Then I realized I was not just imagining it. Someone was actually touching me down there. I opened my eyes just as a piece of dark silk approached my face and blindfolded me.

"Are you feeling this?" I heard Ellie ask from somewhere in front of me while a few fingers caressed my slit. *Were they hers?*

"Yes, I feel it," I said before letting out a long sigh.

"Does it feel good?"

"Yes!" My breath sped up. My body demanded more.

"Later," Ellie said. "It's now time for your massage."

The fingers disappeared and a smell of sandalwood started to envelop me. The sounds of oil squirting out of a bottle and being slapped on skin echoed all around me, then two sets of hands began their work: a person massaged my hands and arms above my head while another massaged my left foot.

I soon felt another pair of hands: this third person caressed my breasts. At first the person's touch was soft, but it quickly became a bit more forceful. A set of wet lips smacked themselves onto mine. A pointy tongue demanded immediate entry, and I parted my mouth. The kisser kindled an urge in me. I didn't know who it was, I could only feel the softness of the skin, the long hair brushing against my face, then the humongous, firm breasts pressed against mine.

It has to be Ellie.

She moved her kisses downward, taking her time around my neck, letting her pointy tongue slide down and tease my nipples as her fingers kneaded my flesh. She made her way to my stomach, then went past it. She traced my newly shaved area with the tip of her fingers. A moan escaped my lips. A little left-over pain from my hair having been pulled stung my flesh, but the cooling cream and the breeze had certainly helped reduce the soreness I expected to feel. For a few seconds, she went away, then her touch resumed. She teased me more and more with her warm breath blowing on my pussy, her tongue licking my folds. All of a sudden, a fingertip prodded my slick opening. The silkiness of someone's long hair brushed against one of my open legs. Other than my guessing that Ellie was the one teasing my pussy, I wasn't sure who was where. However, what they were doing, and the way they were touching me felt marvelous like I was a queen whose every need had to be attended to. Ellie's delightful finger suddenly changed gears and blazed into my wet opening. She pushed it in fully, then slid in another one. Her warm palm cupped below my opening as she stroked my insides with her digits.

And then yet another set of hands joined the party. That fourth person began working my breasts. The person massaging my foot undid my left ankle, lifted it up in the air, and then started kneading my calf. That person was slowly working up toward my thigh. The one massaging my arms had worked his or her way down to my shoulders.

The one who'd been massaging my breasts now suckled on my nipples. The person toying with my pussy—likely Ellie?—was becoming more and more demanding and my body craved it equally. All of it. A hand pushed up my skin to make it taut, announcing my clit as the sole sovereign of my womanhood, then the lick of an agile tongue—a freezing one at that—teased it.

"You like icy kisses?" a woman asked. It was Ellie's voice, and it came from somewhere in front of me.

She's definitely the one between my legs. "I love what you're doing," I said.

"Do you want more?" she asked between licks.

I couldn't resist. "Please!"

She continued licking me and teasing my clit while finger-fucking me. I could feel her entire mouth being buried between my legs, her tongue swirling and exploring my innermost secrets.

"You like that?" she asked.

A moan was all I could muster.

The person who'd been massaging my left leg moved away from me, but a few seconds later, my other ankle was untied and the massage process began again with my right leg. The person who'd been kneading my breasts and suckling on my nipples was now kissing me. I could feel that person's skin being a little rougher than Ellie's lips. I wondered if it was the short muscular masseur or Chakrii, the taller one who had manned the reception earlier. *Or someone else?* Then again, it didn't matter. I had four people caressing me, sending me to cloud nine with their hands, their lips... But, just as Ellie's fingers, tongue, and lips were irreversibly reaching my excitement threshold, she pulled away.

A few seconds later, the soft silky hair that had been brushing against my inner thighs was replaced by the warmth of someone's skin. And then... I felt it.

It was just a poke at first, then more of the man's length slid inside my wet entrance. The hungry mouth that was kissing me swallowed up any moans that escaped my lips as I relished in the filling sensation. While I was blindfolded and couldn't see what was happening, I discarded the idea of a dildo. A warm member filled my hollow and a set of balls slapped my ass as the man buried the full length of his shaft in me. He was kind and slow at first. He gently thrust himself, as if testing the waters or the depth of my womb. Soon thereafter, the cadence increased. I delighted in the feeling of being kissed and massaged and having my breasts caressed while being fucked.

But my wonderful earthly pleasures all stopped at once.

"No!" I yelped like a kid robbed of her ice cream.

"Give us a sec," Ellie's voice replied from in front of me. I heard footsteps nearing my chair. All four of the people had let go of my body. No matter how much I arched my back on the chair, no matter if my pussy was dripping wet, no one appeared to be coming back.

"Come on... Please!" I begged.

A few seconds later, someone walked up to me, finally.

The soft lips that kissed mine along with the ultra-firm, large breasts brushing against my side told me it was Ellie.

She stroked my face gently then untied my wrists. I wanted to pull down my blindfold, but she grabbed my wrists and brought my freed hands to her breasts instead. "Keep your blindfold on for a little while longer," she said before once again locking lips with me and letting her greedy tongue wander in my mouth. A few seconds later, Ellie pulled away from me.

"Now stand up, keep your blindfold on, and I'll guide you."

She pulled me up from the massage chair and dragged me away, very slowly.

The curtains brushed against my skin as she led me out of the room and into another.

"WATCH YOUR STEP," said Ellie.

I slowed down, expecting an obstacle. A second later, my bare foot bumped against a low but fairly soft object in front of me.

"Sit on the mattress," she ordered as she guided me down to a sitting position with both hands.

I once again attempted to remove my blindfold, but Ellie—or someone else—got a hold of my hands and brought them behind my back. I couldn't see anything, but the silky fabric of my open kimono brushed my arms as someone disrobed me. A person started caressing my breasts.

Once my hands were released, I moved them forward, and found Ellie's ultra-firm, naked breasts in front of me. I brought my hands up to her neck and pulled her head closer to mine until our lips met. Her hands gently pushed me over to the left until we both landed sideways, facing each other. We devoured each other's mouth with our heads resting on soft cushions. One of her hands reached down and nudged itself just above my pussy, one of her fingers perfectly positioned to tickle my clit.

I attempted to do the same to her, but she pulled her hips away from me.

"Why?" I asked, wanting once again to pull down my blindfold.

She stopped me. "Not yet," she said, squeezing my hands into hers.

Then something hard and warm poked my ass, successfully distracting me from Ellie. While the person behind me caressed my bum, Ellie repositioned her body away from me—at least it was my best guess since I could no longer feel her body heat—but her lips moved down and started kissing my breasts. I let my hands run through her long silky hair.

Someone squeezed my butt cheeks and then parted them before tracing my crevice all the way to my anus. Ever so gently, something small entered me from behind. But it wasn't a cock, though. I could feel that body part still poking the back of my thigh. *His finger?* Someone circled my inner ring for a while, then probed deeper, slowly, a little bit at a time.

A third person lifted up my right leg and placed my right foot in front of my left knee, turning me into an open oyster ready for the picking. Ellie was still caressing my breasts, and a warm and soft body nudged itself between Ellie and my legs. Unidentified fingers proceeded to look for a hidden pearl in my pussy. That person's touch was delicate, too delicate to be a man's. Then a small breast rubbed against my leg.

Is it the woman who waxed Ellie earlier?

What is this? A foursome? Counting the number of hands touching me was hard with so many delightful sensations ebbing through my body.

The man behind me spoke up. "You feel warm and ready. Take a deep breath," he ordered.

I did. And just then, he pulled out his finger and replaced it with his cock. He must have lubed the hell out of his member because it slid in without any pain. The sound of his lower abdomen slapping against my ass surprised me, but not as much as the feeling inside of me. I hadn't felt so full since... my Costa Rican surf experience. *No, make that the last time I had sex with Matt in Ireland.*

The man behind me stayed still in me for a few seconds while I felt the weight of people shifting in front of me on the mattress. It seemed the man in my ass was the only person left touching me.

But soon, my breasts began to once again receive gentle caresses, and fingers got busy again, entering my wet pussy and tapping me on that oh-so-very-sweet inner spot. The man had set into a rhythm behind me while the unknown fingers fucked my pussy. My right leg started to quiver. I was unable to restrain the movement of my foot; my whole body knew that an orgasm was just around the corner.

Then, the fingers pulled out and a cock took their place. Another one. If I thought I'd been full before, I now knew otherwise. For a few seconds, I was the inner part of a delightful sideway sandwich. But it didn't last long. The man behind me pulled out and spoke up.

"Sit up and ride that cock," he ordered.

Being blindfolded didn't make things easy, but the man in front of me pulled out, and I sat up. Two hands grabbed my shoulders and directed me as I walked on my knees toward the other, whomever that was. My hands helped guide me and I lifted my leg once I felt hips and an erect cock in front of me. Someone guided my right knee to land on the other side of the man's hip. Using only my sense of touch, I lined myself up above his latex-covered dick and slowly lowered myself onto him. At first I rode him slowly, controlling the movement of my hips as my pussy clutched onto his shaft. But then my motions became hastier, driven by my pussy's insatiable hunger.

Moments later, I felt the man behind me caress my ass again, parting a way to return to his previous position, pushing me against the one I was riding. His dick forced his way back into my anus just as I was reaching the threshold of pleasure. Caught off balance and in reaction mode, I moved my hands in front of me to slow down my fall onto the man's chest. But what my hands reached left me flabbergasted.

Large breasts softened my landing just as I came, my insides pulsating out of control.

I let myself rest onto the ultra-firm breasts I'd gotten to know very well over the past few hours. Her lips eagerly found mine while the man behind me kept at it, his balls bouncing against my engorged genitals. The man behind me kept plunging his hard shaft in and out of my ass while my mind was too high on orgasmic chills to deal with what it had just discovered. I lifted up the blindfold and met Ellie's eyes. I kissed her ever so briefly. I pushed away from her with one hand while the other reached down, first to caress her breasts, then to make its way to the base of her shaft, still in me.

"I'm not fully a woman, yet. I just wanted to have one last go with a woman before they performed the other surgery," she said, as if she needed to explain herself.

All of a sudden, Ellie's new breast implants, her hair extensions, and her comfort level with men made sense. Her hand reached down to my clit and she played with it before slowly resuming her cadence with her dick. The man behind me moved one of his hands from my hip to my waist, then grabbed one of my breasts, bringing my back up a bit, against his warm, bare chest. I was a few inches away from Ellie's breasts. I could feel him breathing next to my ear. *Chakrii*, I realized when I saw the small tattoo on his hand. *All 100% man that one.*

I closed my eyes and let myself ride high on the delightful sensations that enveloped my entire body. Chakrii changed his rhythm and depth. He squeezed one of my breasts tighter, then pinched my nipple just a tad too tightly, making my whole body flinch. Then, after a final thrust deep in my ass, he suddenly stopped moving. Ellie's fingers were still busy with my clit while she continued to pound me like it was her cock's last meal, for that it may very well be.

I reopened my eyes and took a hold of Chakrii's hand, which was still firmly squeezing my breast. I brought it down toward my hip again. He slowly pulled himself out of my ass, then stepped away from me, leaving me and Ellie alone in our continuing embrace.

A minute later, Ellie rolled me onto my back, her cock still inside of me. I turned my head and saw other people next to us, naked. The woman who'd waxed Ellie earlier was on her knees, sucking the short, muscular masseur's dick. He was standing up, staring at Ellie and me, his hands on the woman's head, controlling her cadence. Chakrii, who had left me moments ago, had now joined them. He was laying on his back and had squeezed his head between the woman's leg. His hand went up and he began finger-fucking her.

My head dizzy with whatever drugs had been added to my tea, I kept staring at the threesome, hypnotized by the short man's increasingly loud groans. He was about to come, and Ellie's moans above me made it clear she too was approaching that point. Ellie's hand squeezed my cheeks and turned my face forward again, forcing me to make eye contact with her. I stopped looking at the threesome next to us and returned my attention to her. My needs had already been fulfilled, but a faint quiver was telling me I was about to feel another orgasm. With one hand, I reached to squeeze one of her nipples, and with the other, I played with my own clit, making myself quiver more and more until Ellie and I came simultaneously.

She fell forward onto me, our breasts became cushions against which my heart beat out of control. I closed my eyes and relaxed with Ellie still in me.

A moment later, I heard the muscular man grunt as he came. I opened my eyes and looked at them again. The woman, now sitting on Chakrii's face with her throat clear of the short man's dick, soon followed suit and moaned to her heart's content.

I LAY next to Ellie on the mattress after she pulled out of me, a condom securely keeping her come contained.

"Don't worry, we all use protection," Ellie said, as if she'd read my mind. "And he's used the numbing cream on you, so you will likely feel sore tomorrow."

Tomorrow...

Good thing I have an extra day in Bangkok to recover from this new experience, physically and emotionally.

Having had a small orgy with a transgender woman while high on some weird drug-infused tea was certainly a new checkmark on my list (and definitely not one I was planning on ever experiencing in my lifetime).

The past few hours didn't settle my self-questioning about being bisexual.

Am I more of a pansexual?

My pussy didn't seem to care whether it was touched by a man or a woman—or someone in the process of becoming one. Some men got me aroused. Some not. Same was true for women. And then there was Ellie... She definitely got me aroused...

Who knows what label I should assign myself... But does it matter?

It's probably best to step back, turn off my mind, and let my heart and emotions guide me when it comes to intimate encounters and relationships...

PART TWO

MY XXX EXPERIENCE

CHAPTER TWO

ONLY BY EXPERIENCE

THE PLAN

MY STEWARDESS IS DEFINITELY MORE open-minded than I'll ever be. But if she went through what she described in her diary, it just proves that she could be the one to satisfy ALL of my fantasies, even the nasty ones I don't admit to having... even to myself.

But first, I have to find her.

And for that, I'll have to track down Ellie so she can give me more information about the last woman she fucked. She has to remember that, no?

Here are my options:

. . .

OPTION 1: Canvass the airlines for transgender employees.

If only airlines kept those personal details on file, life would be easy... But that would breach some privacy rights and other politically-correct bullshit. Asking around could backfire and instigate a reputation I don't care to have.

Likelihood of success: Close to nil.

OPTION 2: Find Ellie using her language credentials.

Airlines keep records of their employees' language proficiency for obvious reasons, but I'm not sure if *Ellie* is her real name. Doesn't sound Thai to me. And she could have easily changed her name after her final surgery. Too many unknowns to risk wasting my time on this.

Likelihood of success: Low.

OPTION 3: Track down Ellie by talking to the spa employees.

She appears to be a regular at that spa. How many transgender Ellies could be regular clients? And from there, Ellie could hopefully give me my stewardess's name. Sounds like the stewardess shared some personal information with her, so it's not that much of a stretch.

Likelihood of success: Average.

Now, let's just hope my trip to Bangkok doesn't include a tucked-away pig-in-a-blanket.

I'm not interested in that. At all.

WHAT HAPPENED

ARMED WITH HER JOURNAL, a healthy sexual appetite, some curiosity (but not too much), and a whole lot of hope, I took advantage of a two-day layover in BKK/Bangkok to try and track down Ellie, who could hopefully point me to my mystery stewardess.

Bangkok is a large city. Smelly but intriguing. Finding one's way around can be tricky, though. Especially for a non-Thai speaking tourist like me who needs to find a specific location in a city of over eight million inhabitants. However, thanks to a very helpful concierge at my hotel, I did manage to locate the *Shave, Massage, and Beyond Spa*.

About an hour after my initial inquiry, the short

Thai man who was fully fluent in English came back to me with some information. He reported that he'd found it, but that it was a *special spa with full services*, if I was looking for that.

I didn't know if *special spa with full services* was international code for *transgender sex* or simply *massages with happy endings*, but I was hoping for the latter.

The address in hand and a large smile on my face, I hailed a *tuk-tuk* and made my way to the spa with a thick pile of *bahts* in my wallet.

ABOUT THIRTY MINUTES OF LOUD, heavy, and stinky traffic later, I stepped out of the *tuk-tuk* and paid my fearless driver. He nodded at my generous tip and showed me the largest smile I'd seen in a long time, complete with a couple of gaps where teeth had gone missing. I returned my wallet in the pocket of my khaki shorts, which were damp with sweat and probably saturated with pollution. The same was true for my gray T-shirt. But a nearby food stand offered an aroma that made me salivate and instantly forget about the humid climate. There was food everywhere in this city, but I wasn't here to eat. Food could wait. I was here on a mission. An important recon mission.

I looked up to the big white sign my driver had pointed to before leaving. The name of the spa wasn't written in English, but the squiggly Thai characters on the oasis-themed signage matched what my hotel concierge had scribbled on the piece of paper I held.

"Here's to nothing," I said to myself as I opened the dark glass door and stepped into the much cooler reception area, triggering a chime in the process.

An overpowering smell of incense made me sneeze just as a short man welcomed me in. I missed his first name, but it wasn't Chakrii. *Could he be the short muscular man who had taken part in the orgy with my stewardess?* I couldn't really ask him that question right now, but I wouldn't have described him as muscular. I was probably twice as heavy as he was. But then again, I spent a fair amount of time at the pool and at the gym, and I was definitely built on a bigger frame than he was.

He smiled at me and offered me a list of services printed in English on a narrow sheet of white paper. From my limited experience with spas, everything offered on their leaflet seemed legit. No extra-curricular services there, but that was no surprise. As expected, there was a Thai massage on the list of services, but from what I'd learned before while researching Thai spas online (hoping to find the right one), those massages were normally done with your clothes on. After a few more seconds, I settled on the deep-tissue, therapeutic massage, claiming that my back and neck hurt from spending too much time in front of a computer. Then, realizing I wasn't necessarily targeting anything physically close to a happy ending, I added that my legs also hurt from running.

"Do you want a man or a woman to give you your massage?" he asked.

"A woman, if at all possible," I said, hoping that it could possibly be the short, small-breasted woman who'd taken part in the orgy. Or that she could end the massage on a happy note.

He nodded and then guided me to the waiting area before returning to his reception desk.

I sat quietly while observing the rest of the entrance. There was a fountain in the center of the hall, just like my mystery stewardess had described. I looked at my sweaty T-shirt and hoped to be taken to the communal shower next...

Maybe a couple of women would already be in there?

JUST AS MY brain finished adding intricate details to the imaginary tall, beautiful, naked women in the shower I was looking forward to seeing, I was taken out of my daydream by someone addressing me.

I turned to look at the short but very busty woman who had come to greet me. She was in her late twenties or early thirties. *So much for randomly finding the woman from the orgy! Guess it wasn't in the cards for today.*

The woman in front of me wore a very short white uniform, just as the stewardess had described in her journal. However, I was surprised at the amount of cleavage she showed. Sure, a nip-slip wasn't just waiting to happen—like with the maids' uniforms in my special Irish castle—but the visible portions of her cappuccino-colored mounds were still very pleasant to the eye. Her outfit reminded me of a slutty nurse uniform a woman-friend had once worn (very briefly) for Halloween. I don't think we'd made it to the party that night. The memory of what had ensued was enough to make my dick twitch in my shorts. *But that was then and I'm here now.*

I got up and followed the tiny-assed woman past some long curtains and we arrived in the shower room that looked just like what I had imagined (save for the naked women—those were missing). Not much had changed since my stewardess's journal entry. That was probably a good sign. At least she hadn't written her entries decades ago...

I followed the short woman's instructions the instant she left.

I stripped down to nothing, placed my wallet and clothes in one of the small lockers, then hopped under the stream of running water. While I showered, a couple of people took a passing peek. But I could care less. I had nothing to hide. In fact, my cock, even when flaccid, normally appreciated all of the attention it could get.

Once all of the sweat and pollution had come off my skin, I stepped out of the shower and dried myself off before picking one of the longer silk robes hanging from the rack.

THE WOMAN who'd brought me to the shower magically reappeared the instant I tied the robe around my waist.

Guess she was hiding somewhere and looking at me the entire time? Good for her.

She took me to a small circular room with only one massage table and one large fan on a pedestal. There were no walls per se, only curtains. The massage table looked normal to me, nothing like the weird contraption the stewardess had described in her diary. But it had a pedal underneath it, probably a hydraulic jack.

"Please. Lie naked with face down," the woman

said in a staccato with her strong Thai accent before exiting the room.

After looking around for a place to hang my robe and finding nothing—not even a hook—I dropped it on the floor. I lay down and placed my face in the wide, barely padded opening. It wasn't like that of the regular massage tables I'd been on before. My head hung lower than normal. I'd barely lost any of my vision field, save for what was behind me and above the table, obviously. But the weird hole was still comfortable, and it was all that mattered.

A few seconds later, some strange, soothing, Enya-like music speckled with the rings of singing bowls began to air just loud enough to cover the sound of the oscillating fan near me. The woman returned to the room shortly thereafter, rolling a small tray in front of her.

"Your neck and back hurt?" she asked while placing a towel over my ass.

"Yes, and my legs, too," I replied.

My vantage point was odd, but I quickly got used to it. I could see her standing next to the tray. Based on the odor that tickled my nose and made me want to sneeze, she had lit a stick of incense.

Her bare foot then came toward me, and she pumped up the pedal to lift the table.

For a split second, I thought I got a glance at her pussy, but then she walked away and returned to her tray.

She picked up a brown bottle and squirted out some of its aromatic oil. After rubbing her hands together, she walked closer to me, bringing her tray along. With another squirt, she spilled the cool oil directly onto my back, then she traced circles on my skin to spread it. She slowly made her way around the table. It was so high—and her uniform was so short—that every now and then, whenever she reached out across my body, her white uniform would ride up, exposing her shaved pussy. No landing strip on display there, nothing at all. I could have been fooled and assumed I was looking at a very young girl, but I clearly remembered seeing the face of a woman who was at least in her late twenties.

A guy could never be blamed for looking at naked female parts while in plain view, but getting a hard-on while lying face down wasn't the most comfortable thing in the world. I lifted my hips and used one hand to nudge my erect dick into a more bearable position as discreetly as I could.

"You like?" she asked, untangling knots in my back with her vigorous hand motions.

Guess my readjustment wasn't as smooth and swift as I thought...

Considering I likely wasn't the first man who'd been turned on by her intermittently exposed pussy, I played along, wondering how this scenario would unfold.

"Yes, of course," I said. "You're good. How long have you been giving massages?"

She returned closer to my head, once again offering me a good vantage point of her pussy as she worked on the knots I really did have at the base of my neck. "Few years..."

Asking for a precise number probably fell in that large basket of inappropriate questions women didn't like to be asked, like their age, weight, or number of sexual partners. "Do you mainly massage women or men?"

"Men and women," she said, not expanding any more on the topic.

And people who are simultaneously a man and a woman? Or transitioning from one to the other? My thoughts alone took care of my erection, so I was once again lying comfortably on the table.

After undoing all of the knots in my back, she

moved to my arms. She worked her way from my shoulders down to my fingers. At first, my hand rested on her shoulder, but she gradually moved backward and my fingers landed on the exposed part of her breasts. I hesitated for a second, then figured it was worth a shot. I wiggled my fingers lightly, brushing them against her exposed flesh. A second later, she popped a button off her dress and asked again, "You like?"

So, this is how happy endings were offered?

I twisted my elbow around and flat out grabbed one of her breasts out of her bra before giving it a good squeeze.

"I see you like this, mister," she said. "Do you want more?" she asked, moving out of my reach.

"Sure," I said, my dick once again reaffirming its uncomfortable enthusiasm.

A second later, she moved to the front of the table, then knelt below my head. My masseuse unbuttoned her top and let both of her gorgeous cappuccino breasts pop out of her bra.

Too firm and perky to be real, but glorious for sure.

"You like?" she asked again. Her delicate hands decorated with hot-red fingernails started caressing her exposed breasts. I couldn't see her eyes, but her smile was that of an innocent young girl. However,

I didn't let myself be fooled by it. She was an experienced sex trade worker who knew how to get a big tip.

"What else can you do to relax me?" I asked, curious as to how far massage parlors took it in Thailand.

She stopped caressing her tits, then unbuttoned her uniform some more. Although my view point was perfect, my erection made the whole thing near painful to watch laying face down. So I turned around on the table and my erection bounced to celebrate its newfound freedom. I sat in the middle of the table, then swung my legs off to the side while she stood up and repositioned herself in front of me.

With one of her delicate fingers, she slowly traced the sensitive underside of my cock. "I see you like this," she repeated again.

"What kind of... services do you offer?" I asked.

She winked and her smile grew even bigger. "Anything you want, big mister. If you pay, I give you."

"What about orgies?"

She let out a giggle and feigned being offended. "Orgies? A lot of money, mister."

"But they happen here? Sometimes?"

"No say," she said before literally not being able to say a word as she bent forward and swallowed my dick in her mouth.

I parted my thighs and slid to the edge of the table.

She was good. Just the right amount of pressure, just the right tempo.

Damn. Can't think. Must continue asking. Must track Ellie down.

When she slid her mouth off of my dick for a second, I finally mustered enough concentration and blood flow to my brain to ask, "Do you know Ellie?"

"Ellie? What Ellie?" she said, her eyes locking onto mine as she massaged my balls with one hand and gave me a hand-job with the other.

"I don't know her last name. A *he-she*. Used to be a man, now a woman."

She squeezed my balls upon hearing my words.

"Ow!" I yelped.

She released her grasp. "Sorry... No news from Ellie in long time."

"So you know her?"

She nodded. "Why you look for her?"

"I'm trying to track down a friend of hers."

"Maybe I help," she said, tilting her head and stepping back.

"What do you know?"

"Ten times the price, I tell you everything."

I pondered for a second. The massage wasn't that expensive anyway. Her offer seemed fair, but I knew bartering was part of the way people did business here.

"Here's what: Happy ending with you and another woman in the shower, and you tell me everything you know. Then I'll pay ten times the price."

She started buttoning up her uniform again. "Fifteen times and it's deal."

"Twelve times with a guarantee that I'll make you come."

She pursed her lips for a few seconds. Her stare went from my eyes to my cock, then back to my eyes.

"Okay, big mister. Deal. I go get Anong."

She tucked her breasts in her bra before disappearing behind the curtain and leaving me alone to contemplate my situation for a second.

Not a bad deal. She could know enough to help me. And if not, I'll get a threesome with two small Asian pussies. Can't be bad, right?

4:12 P.M.

WHEN I SAW my short masseuse return with a gorgeous, slender, and slightly taller woman by her side, I knew I'd made the right call.

This other woman must be Anong.

She too wore a uniform that was two sizes too small, leaving two-thirds of her small breasts a secret to be uncovered and her pussy a stretch from being exposed. Unfortunately, I also had to rule her out of being the other woman who had taken part in the orgy. She was too tall for that. But that didn't matter. I had two gorgeous Thai women at my mercy, and I was going to make the most of it, no doubt about it!

I jumped down from where I sat and walked toward the two women. "We're done with the massage part of the program," I said before wrapping my hands around their waists. "Let's hit the shower."

My erection led the way to the room on the other side of the curtains.

The water was still running although no one was using the shower, and an urge to see what the stewardess had experienced came over me. I wanted to see these beautiful women get wet with their clothes on. I wanted them to soap themselves up in front of me and then explore each other's body.

I brought my gorgeous ladies to the outer rim of the shower basin and they both started to unbutton their uniform dresses. "No, with your clothes on," I said, which made them stop disrobing immediately. "Come with me."

Without arguing, protesting, or even displaying a hint of a frown, they followed me to the nearest stream of water.

I sure love women who play along.

After a few seconds under the stream, it became clear that the taller woman was braless. The dark circles of her areolae and her tiny, pointy nipples poked through the white fabric of her wet uniform. *Small, perky, young, natural breasts.* It had been a while since I'd seen a pair of those.

The older, shorter woman pulled a long metal pin out of her hair, which she then flung behind her. She shook her head, tossing her now-free, long black hair sideways a couple of times before leaning backward to wet it. Once it was drenched, she took a step back and let the stream of water hit her on the chest. She undid the rest of the uniform buttons that covered her bra and then pulled her augmented breasts out in the open.

Saying she was a sight for sore eyes—not that my eyes were sore at all—would have been an understatement. But just when I thought the view couldn't get better, my short and busty masseuse bunched the bottom of her dress around her waist, exposing her bald pussy. Anong took a few steps back, away from the water stream. A wide smile illuminated her face as her stare repeatedly went up and down, eyeing her coworker's body.

Anong closed the one-foot gap that stood between her and my short masseuse, and they kissed under the running water. But it wasn't just a peck. They devoured each other's lips and mouth.

Anong's hands were all over my short masseuse's fake tits. I took a few steps to the left, taking in the view while I grabbed a hold of my cock. The masseuse's hands went for Anong's ass and lifted the bottom of her uniform to expose her bum before grabbing it. Seemed Anong too had skipped putting on panties this morning. Her small, round ass was as beautiful as they came. From where I stood right at that moment, her pussy still remained a mystery.

I made my way to them, my hand gently pumping my cock, while I pondered how to best play this threesome. I had promised the older woman an orgasm, and I wasn't one to make empty promises. She was going to get it, but... Anong's young ass tempted me more than anything right now. It was a perfect peach, ripe for my poking.

I walked to them and moved the masseuse's hands away from my plump prize. It was as firm as I'd imagined it would be. I massaged and parted her cheeks. I squeezed the hell out of her flesh. I was about to poke her when the masseuse broke away from Anong and knelt down in front of me.

The older woman took hold of my wild beast and started licking it. Her mouth was truly gifted, so I let her warm me up.

I released Anong's ass, then spun her around.

Her dark brown eyes looked down the instant I tried to make eye contact. I lifted her chin, hoping she'd look at me, but she didn't. Instead, she pulled down her uniform, hiding her pussy before I could even glimpse at it. Her eyes went to my cock next. Or was she staring at the older woman sucking me?

First time she's seen a cock this size? Shy? Or does she prefer women?

I traced an imaginary line that followed the water's path as it streamed down Anong's uniform, from her neck to the hem of her skirt, just past her still mysterious pussy. I started unbuttoning her dress slowly. She let me, her arms hanging by her sides while she watched my masseuse repeatedly guzzle my cock. Anong wasn't pushing me away, but she wasn't encouraging me either. I grabbed her breasts through the soaking wet fabric and squeezed their natural goodness. I reached down to grab the hem of her skirt, and I lifted it to see if her pussy was as gorgeous as her ass. A lightning bolt greeted my stare. *That's different.* I reached out to the soap dispenser and pumped out a handful of the aromatic gel. I rubbed my hands together to create foam before taking them to Anong's breasts. Then, as though I couldn't help myself, my hands erred south to tickle the tip of that lightning rod.

At that precise moment, as though my touching her clit had activated a switch in her brain, Anong started to participate. She pulled her soaking wet uniform over her head and tossed it away from us. The beautiful Anong now stood butt naked next to me and the one who was blowing me. I wasn't going to last long if the older woman continued to use her mouth like that.

I looked around the room and realized the edge of the tiled shower area could be wide enough to fuck on. I gently pushed away the head of the one blowing me, and like the true gentleman that I am, I offered her my hand so she could get up and off of her knees.

A second later, once on her feet, she took off her uniform as well. I pointed toward the rim and the two naked women looked at each other.

"One minute," the older one said before walking away.

She came back three seconds later with a towel and a bunch of condoms. She spread the towel on the wide ledge, then lay her bare back on it. The younger woman came and squatted over her face, at the perfect height to be licked by the other woman. They definitely offered a nice, electrifying view for me. *Her southern lightning 'do sure is nice, but her ass...*

"Turn around," I ordered Anong.

She obeyed. After straightening her legs and stepping over the ledge to turn away from me, she realigned herself with the other woman's face. I stared at her sublime ass as she lowered her pussy over her friend's mouth.

While she licked Anong, the older woman touched herself, her fingers swarming and circling her clit like hyperactive bees. Her legs fell on both sides of the wall, her pussy rested wide open for the world to see. I unwrapped the first condom and protected myself before making my way to her. She obviously knew how to warm herself up. Her implants pointed to the sky and I squeezed their perfect semi-spherical shapes while admiring the most perfect ass hovering a mere foot away. That visual simulation was like dumping gas on my already blazing libido, so I sat on the ledge in front of the masseuse's pussy.

The older woman sure had good balancing skills to keep herself from falling off on either side of the eight-inch-wide rim. To ensure I wouldn't mess up her balancing act, I carefully lifted, then rested the older woman's legs over mine one at a time. Her calves dangled past my thighs as I moved forward and brought my knees to the floor. Carefully—I didn't want her to fall off—I plunged my cock into her bare pussy. It glided inside her like butter on steaming bread. Either she was really loose or really turned on. *Maybe she has a thing for blond-haired Caucasian men? Or Anong?* I increased my pounding slowly, ensuring I wasn't going to throw her off balance, then my hands reached out to Anong's ass. I parted her firm, fleshy cheeks and caressed her crack. The masseuse's tongue was taking care of Anong's pussy, so I moved my attention to her taint. *It ain't quite pussy, t'ain't quite ass.* I dipped a finger in the water that had accumulated in the basin, then brought it to the rim of her ass. I circled it, then poked the tip of my finger into her dark hole.

Anong yelped. I took it out, then slowly pushed it back in, this time, deeper. As I shoved it in farther, she moaned and straightened her back. *Guess you like ass-play, dear? Coming right up.*

The third time around, she moaned even louder, this time twisting at the hip in an attempt to look my way.

"More!" Anong ordered. "Give me more fingers!"

*I'm a man who gives women what they want—at least while doing them—*so I added a second finger. I finger-fucked Anong's ass while I cock-fucked her friend's pussy, watching the large implants bounce between Anong's beautiful ass and me.

A few seconds later, Anong's moans skipped a few notches on the Richter's scale, and her screams became that of a winding ambulance siren. She bent her body forward, away from me. She landed flat on the ledge, past her friend's head. So I had to let go of her ass and concentrate on the older woman.

She, too, appeared to have had enough stimulation to reach her pleasure threshold. Now that her mouth was free from Anong's pussy, I started hearing her groans. Her left knee bucked a second before her entire body started convulsing into waves of pleasure, contracting against my shaft as I stayed inside her.

I paused there for a few seconds, feeling her heartbeat through her engorged genitals before pulling out. I still had a few minutes in me, so I carefully detangled my legs from the masseuse's limbs then got up. Anong's glorious ass was right there. So I quickly washed my hands and traded my condom for a new one before walking toward her. This time, she looked me in the eyes. Then she looked at my cock and smiled. Without saying a word, she looked back toward her ass and parted her cheeks.

Clear enough!

Her friend had since gotten up, so I now had room to sit behind Anong. I rode the ledge just behind her ass and, after parting her cheeks, pushed my dick into her plumpness. Her ass was tight. She squealed—joyfully of course—as I finally plunged my full length into her. I bent forward and wrapped my body behind her, getting a hold of her small breasts. The older woman had already made her come, so I didn't worry too much whether or not I would. Although I would never admit to this aloud, at forty-two, I no longer had the endurance I used to have. Pleasing two women in one go now involved a lot more strategy, but I wasn't one to give up so easily. I lifted my hips to ensure I wouldn't put extra weight on her tiny body, then let go of one of her tits to reach for her clit. Seemed she'd beat me to it. Instead, I dipped one finger then two into her wet pussy. She rubbed herself so quickly and forcefully that her wrists forced my fingers out of her. Her moans began to get louder and I knew I wasn't going to last a minute. A few more deep thrust into her ass and we both came. Her high-pitch squeals nearly deafened me—and most certainly covered up my own ecstatic grunts.

Once my bliss came to an end, I pulled out of Anong's fantastic ass and remembered that these women possibly held useful information about my mysterious woman, or at least her friend Ellie.

4:50 P.M.

I SLAPPED Anong's gorgeous ass as she got up, and she flashed me a shy smile. Her cheeks were bright red.

I turned to my masseuse, who was busy picking up their wet uniforms from the floor a few feet away from me.

"So, you promised me information about Ellie," I said as I walked closer to her. "I'm looking for a friend Ellie brought here. She had sex with her and other people here."

The masseuse raised her brows. "Ellie has lots of friends and lots of sex."

"It was while she still had a dick," I clarified. "She was with a Caucasian woman."

The older woman's eyes went up, "Ah! I know who you mean."

"Do you know her name?"

"No. No name," she said while shaking her head.

"Do you know what she looks like?"

"You say she your friend and you no know how she looks?"

"I found something that belongs to her, and I'm trying to find her so I can return it, okay?"

"More than we agreed. Fifteen times the price."

"Fifteen times and you answer all my questions about that woman and Ellie?"

"Okay, mister," she said before turning away to Anong. "You go now, prepare for next client."

And just like that, Anong left. I looked at her gorgeous ass as she walked away, out of the room.

"Anong no knows Ellie. She starts working here after," she explained.

"So, describe that other woman for me. Tall? Short? Fat? Pretty? Ugly?"

"Taller than me and Anong. Pretty. Brown wavy hair. Medium breasts, large ass. All white women have large asses."

At least the descriptions remained fairly consistent, but a large ass? Could I really have been obsessed by a woman who may not be that attractive? I tried to clarify how large her ass was by putting my hands about two feet apart. She moved them closer by about three-quarters of a foot.

Definitely not the tiny Asian ass that had just left the room, but it wasn't that bad, assuming she had the right curves to match. But trying to find an average looking, brown-haired woman among the sea of stewardesses out there would be difficult. Red hair or huge breasts would have stood out a bit more. But at least she was sexy enough to have sex with other women... and open-minded enough to do it with a transgender woman as well. That had to count for something.

"Did she speak with an accent of any kind?"

"American, like you."

"From the South?" I asked, hopeful to narrow it down a little.

"Don't know. I do massage. I'm not language teacher."

"Fair enough. What else can you tell me about her, or about Ellie?"

"You get dressed, I go get a picture of Ellie."

A few minutes later, I had hopped in the shower again, dried myself off, gotten dressed, and then returned to the reception area to wait for my masseuse and her photo. Because she still had to appear, I also dug out my wallet and pulled out the agreed-upon money to settle my bill.

I had just double-counted my pile of *bahts* when my masseuse appeared with a worn out photo of her and Ellie, both sporting large smiles and sexy tops that put on display their large implants.

"After my surgery," she said, pointing at her breasts.

"Can I keep this?" I asked, pointing at the photo she held.

She shook her head and sent angry looks at me. "No, my photo." She brought it against her chest, hiding it from me.

"Could I snap a picture of your photo with my phone?"

She raised her shoulders and tilted her head.

I took a few more bills out of my wallet and added them to the pile I was about to hand her.

"Okay," she said, taking my money then handing me her photo.

I dug out my phone and accessed the right app. "Do you know which airline Ellie works for?" I asked as I photographed her old picture.

"No more information," she said, shaking her

head. Her smile had disappeared from her face. She was busy counting my money.

I knew when to stop pushing my luck and other people's patience. I gave her back her photograph, thanked her, and then headed back to my hotel room, unsure where to go from here.

BACK IN THE comfort of my air-conditioned room, after a stop by a food stand to pick up the most delicious pad thai I'd ever eaten, I threw myself on the bed.

What a day!

I lifted my hip from the mattress, then dug out my phone from my back pocket. I made my way to my photos and then looked at Ellie with my masseuse. Ellie sure was a good-looking transgender woman. Delicate nose, beautiful eyes, luscious lips... And those tits! She could have easily fooled me. Unsure how I would have reacted to seeing her dick, though. *Anger? Confusion? Repulsion? All of the above?*

No one could ever convince me to trade in my cock, no matter the price tag. For Ellie—or anyone else born as a male—to be willing to go through that sort of life-altering surgery, there had to be a monumental reason behind it. I doubt any man would be willing to lose his dick just to get a thrill. Or to be able to grab boobs 24/7. *What was it? Tremendous discomfort in one's skin?*

I shook my head, not wanting to waste a second more on this topic. It didn't matter anyway. What mattered was that I now had Ellie's headshot.

How can I try to track her down? Through company records?

But which airline does she work for?

All major airlines flew to Bangkok or had a partner airline that did.

Maybe I'll encounter her in person one day, in a random airport, by sheer luck...

Talk about the slimmest of odds...

My eyes went to the masseuse that accompanied Ellie on the photo. She had said something about her surgery. Could it be that *she* was the small-breasted woman who'd taken part in the stewardess's orgy?

And with that thought, I closed my eyes and mentally relived my afternoon shower adventures, but turning it into a foursome that included my mystery stewardess.

NEXT STEPS

I RE-READ her next journal entry, and what she wrote about her experience in France just proves to me that she's a woman. *Take that, Bob, for your idea that it's a man playing an elaborate prank on me!* Even if a man had somehow forged the experiences I was able to track down so far (by paying off the people I spoke to for example), no man would have ever gone through such a roller-coaster of emotions and then written about it.

Messed up shit? Don't know, but it's definitely not what I'd consider to be a regular fun trip to France.

Can't judge her, though. Everyone has their ups and downs.

Who's to say that her way of dealing with them wasn't the best under her circumstances?

But maybe she made a mistake by blabbing so much in her diary.

Maybe she left me enough clues to track her down this time...

TO BE CONTINUED...

...IN PART 7 of *The Stewardess's Diary*, available at most major book retailers.

The complete episodic novel is also available in one (thick) paperback with exclusive author's notes about the series and what inspired each episode.

ABOUT THE AUTHOR

S.M. Pratt is a single woman traveling the world on her own, living in the moment, looking for more than love, and always trying out new things. Fun adventures and unique cultural experiences are always at the top of her agenda, no matter the country she happens to be visiting.

She would love to quit her day job and write full-time. You can help her write the next story faster by purchasing her books and/or giving her five-star reviews. Without your support, she's invisible and unable to make a living doing what she loves, which is creating what you love to read.

If you haven't done so already, please join her private reader group for previews, exclusive offers, and more. It's free: https://smpratt.com

For more information:
smpratt.com
info@smpratt.com